Tips for Reading Together

Children learn best when reading is fun.

- Talk about the title and the pictures on the cover.
- Discuss what you think the story might be about.
- Read the story together, inviting your child to read as much of it as they can.
- Give lots of praise as your child reads, and help them when necessary.
- Try different ways of helping if they get stuck on a word. For example, get them to say the first sound of the word, or break it into chunks, or read the whole sentence again, trying to guess the word. Focus on the meaning.
- Have fun finding the hidden hiking boots.
- Re-read the story later, encouraging your child to read as much of it as they can.

Children enjoy re-reading stories and this helps to build their confidence.

Have fun!

Find the 10 hiking boots hidden in the pictures.

Mountain Rescue

Written by Cynthia Rider

Illustrated by Alex Brychta

OXFORD
UNIVERSITY PRESS

Biff was showing Wilma her new
music box.

"It's like a little house," said Wilma.

Biff opened the box and the music
began to play. Suddenly, the magic
key began to glow.

The magic took Biff and Wilma
to a mountain railway station.
"The station looks just like my
music box," said Biff.

There was a big wooden horn
at the station. A boy called Max told
them that it was used to send for the
Mountain Rescue helicopter.

"My Uncle Hans flies the helicopter," he said. "He's taking me to see an eagle's nest today. You can come with us."

The children got into a train. It
took them higher up the mountain.
Uncle Hans was waiting at the
station.

"Hi Max," said Uncle Hans. "I'm glad some of your friends have come with you."

Uncle Hans and the children went
up a steep track. They saw some
people climbing a steep rock.

"That looks scary!" said Biff.

Just then, Uncle Hans's phone
rang. "I have to go back, but you
can see the eagle's nest from here,"
he said.

The eagle was sitting on her nest.
Suddenly, she squawked and flew
into the sky.

"A man has climbed up to the
nest!" said Biff. "He's putting the
eagle's egg into his bag."

"Put that egg back!" shouted
Wilma.

The man looked up. He saw the
children watching him and started
to run.

"He's going to the station," said
Max. "Quick! Let's follow him and
get the egg back." They slipped and
scrambled down the steep path.

At last, they reached the station.
Wilma ran up to the man.

"We saw you take an egg from the
eagle's nest," she said.

The man was angry. "I didn't take
an egg," he said, and he opened his
bag. There was no egg inside.

Suddenly, there was a shout.

"One of the climbers has fallen!" said Max. "We must call the Mountain Rescue Team."

Wilma ran to blow the horn, but
the man tried to stop her.

"Give me that horn!" he shouted,
but Wilma pulled it away from him.

The Mountain Rescue helicopter flew into the sky. Everyone cheered as the climber was lifted to safety.

The helicopter landed and Max
showed Uncle Hans the eagle's egg.
"We must put the egg back before
it gets cold," said Uncle Hans.

Uncle Hans climbed up to the nest
and put the egg back. The eagle saw
the egg and flew back to her nest.

Three big feathers floated gently
down to the children.

"The eagle is saying thank you,"
said Biff, as the magic key glowed.

"Look! There's a wooden horn
on your music box now," said
Wilma. "How did it get there?"

"It must be magic," smiled Biff.

Think about the story

What was
the big wooden horn
used for?

How do
you think the children
felt when the man
showed them his
empty bag?

Why did Max
wrap the egg in
his jacket?

How would
you feel if you saw
someone steal
something?

A maze

Help Uncle Hans put the egg back.

More books for you to enjoy

Level 1: Getting Ready

Level 2: Starting to Read

Level 3: Becoming a Reader

Level 4: Building Confidence

Level 5: Reading with Confidence

OXFORD
UNIVERSITY PRESS

Great Clarendon Street,
Oxford OX2 6DP

Written by Cynthia Rider based
on original characters created by
Roderick Hunt and Alex Brychta
Text © Cynthia Rider 2008
Illustrations © Alex Brychta 2008
This edition published 2010

First published 2008

Read at Home Series Editors:
Kate Ruttle, Annemarie Young

British Library Cataloguing
in Publication Data available

ISBN: 9780198387725

10 9 8 7 6 5 4 3 2 1

Printed in China by Imago

Have more fun with Read at Home